I am an ARO PUBLISHING THIRTY WORD BOOK
My thirty words are:

a	is	snake
camping	like	soak
do	make	space
eat	mistake	spot
feet	new	tents
fence	our	that
fishing	place	to
game	pet	we (we've)
got	race	what
hike	short	with

ISBN 0-89868-181-2 — Library Bound
ISBM 0-89868-182-0 — Soft Bound

MY FIRST THIRTY WORD BOOKS

My First Camping Trip

Story by Julia Allen
Pictures by Bob Reese

 ARO PUBLISHING

What

to do?

A game

that is new!

That place is

our camping space.

We make our tents

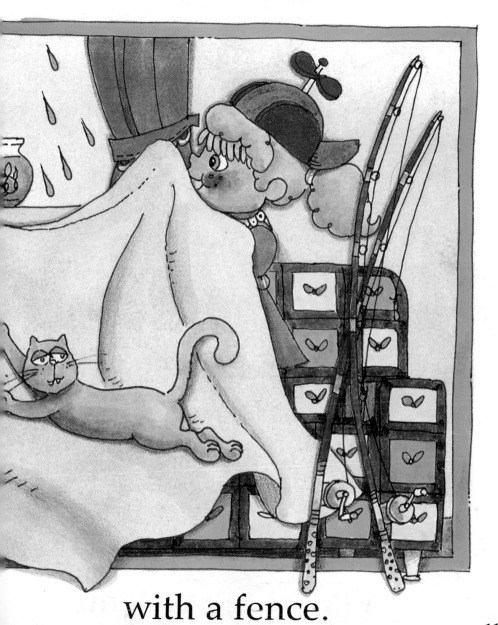

with a fence.

A fishing spot

is what we've got.

A short hike

is what we like.

To pet a snake

is a mistake.

We like to race to our

camping place.

We like

to eat.

We like to

soak our feet.